Dancing with Broken Bones

DR. VERNITA BALDWIN

Dancing with Broken Bones

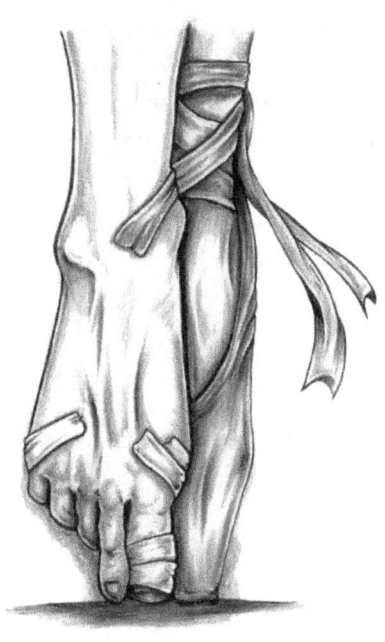

*"Life is like a dance. You rise, you fall, you spin, and you crawl.
But like the dance, life is beautiful, sometimes you are sharp and rough.
Other days you are smooth and graceful. Life is a dance where the
beginning is the hardest but when you start to flow you glow. Don't over
analyze it, just do it. Be who you are at the deepest core of your being."*

~*Regina Malabago*~

Table of Contents

Dedication

This Labor of Love
Is
Dedicated To
The Beats of My Heart
Melvin "Trae" Baldwin, III
And
Anthony Tremayne Baldwin

Cover Design	**C. Cole Vergara**
Photographer	**LynTracey Images**

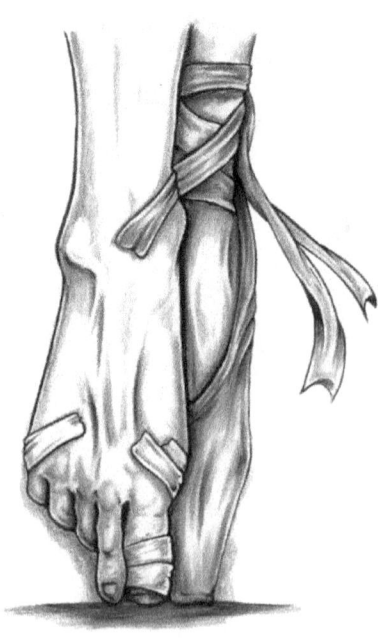

Foreword

*D*ance is a unique art form in which performers tell a story through movement and emotion. Feelings are transferred into expression from the slightest to the most abrupt ways. A gesture as simple as a head turn can convey an essence that makes the Dance palpable. A series of turns can heighten emotions and increase the heart rate with joy or anticipation. Dr. Baldwin has used the metaphor of Dance to escort us through her journey. Those who know this woman recognize the symbolism of this book's title, "Dancing With Broken Bones," as a nod to the training, perseverance, performance, and tragedy that has been her life journey. If you have seen a picture of a ballerina's feet outside her pointe shoes, the pain, and trials required to wear that costume to honor it becomes evident. The bruised, calloused, bloody, and unattractive in every societal norm, the ballerina barefoot shows her story.

For dancers, the stage and the studio keep calling us back. The commitment to training, to pushing your technique, to perfecting each step is what we define as passion. The stage, the connection with the audience, and the adrenaline from the lights, costumes, and performance fill our souls.

If you think about it, we have all 'danced with broken bones' at some point in our lives. Those moments when life knocks you down, but time slowly comes to heal that wound, and before you know it, it's showtime again.

In its purest essence, Dance connects mind, body, and spirit. It's humanity. One of the most extended established art forms influencing every century is ancestry, geography, and now modern-day technology. Dances are woven into every part of traditional customs, life milestones, and family lineage. We find Dance in how the wind blows the trees, how a toddler discovers music, and how a chef moves about the prep line of a busy kitchen. We can find Dance in our morning routine of moving about the kitchen to prepare a meal, and we find Dance in Dr. Baldwin's interpretation of a little girl who watched her Momma and Grandmother run a café. The foundation of Dance starts at the barre, in the studio. But the foundation for our own story begins in the memories we hold closest.

May you all have the strength to Dance.

Katie Sheehan-Smith

Dance Instructor

York County (VA) School of the Arts

Introduction

*D*ance is defined as a performing art-form consisting of purposefully selected sequences of human movement. Other forms of human movement are sometimes said to have a dance-like quality, including martial arts, gymnastics, cheerleading, figure skating, synchronized swimming, marching bands, and many other types of athletics. Antonia Grove, Artistic director, Probe Magazine asserts that "dance communicates in a way that no other art form can…" She says, "in my opinion it has a unique ability to reach people viscerally, energetically and poetically in a way that is both primitive and sophisticated." "It can be as simple or as complex as is needed…It remains for me a beautifully abstracted and intangible form of communication, and in this world where we strive for knowledge, clarity and a quick diagnosis of situations, it retains an essence of mystery."

The NBC Network featured a show called the World of Dance. On Tuesday, January 26, 2019, the junior girls dance group category featured a solo dancer named Nia. Nia had selective mutism (she didn't speak!). But...dance is where she speaks! It was something about Nia that struck a deep puncture in my own shaky dance legs of life. I recall a dear friend and sorority sister who has faced her own battle dance with breast cancer. Some ten or so years ago, she mailed me the sweetest stuffed elephant adorned with a red and white polka-dot jumpsuit. She named her Nia. How ironic. Nia, a girl's name, is pronounced NEE-ah. It is of Gaelic and Swahili origin and the meaning of Nia is "lustrous; goal, purpose, brilliance."

As a little colored girl born in the Deep South in the mid 50's to a young mother who had just turned 17 years old, I was born and named Vernita Lucas. Yet in retrospect, I was Nia. I was Nia because I was seen but not allowed to be heard. I was Nia because I wanted to dance with purpose and brilliance but had no voice. The only person who was compassionate enough to hear my voice and persuade me to dance was my granddaddy. Granddaddy always had the time and the patience to...listen to my voice and watch me dance. Whether I talked about my fatigue from dancing with the dishes in the sink at the cafe (aka Ethel's Tea Room) or dancing as a babysitter while watching my little twin brothers as a child myself. I danced as Nia! Yet had no voice. When I was young, children were seen and not heard. Your thoughts didn't matter. Your voice didn't matter. My constant pipe dream was to take dance lessons and become a professional dancer whose voice would be echoed through the dance motions of life.

Dance classes weren't the normal extracurricular activity for black youth living in the segregated South in the 1950s and 1960s. Yet my mother EJ and grandmother Nellie's Juke-Joint, Ethel's Tea Room, served as my dance stage. Inside the Juke-Joint it was sizzling hot on the dance floor. Dance movements ranged from the fast Boogaloo to the slow and sultry "Slow Drag." The "Slow Drag" was an up-close and personal slow-grinding kind of dance movement that alluded to sexual healing. In the atmosphere of emotional tests, trials, and personal tribulations, stress and tension were dispersed on the dance floor. Testimonials likely fluctuated from hurt and harm to sexual healing. Nia witnessed her mother and grandmother dance as Negro and female entrepreneurs working in the heat and humidity of a dancing Juke Joint. Those two phenomenal women could have coined the term "sweat equity." They danced with vigor, with class, and with determination, setting an unforgettable example for a little skinny leg and all aspiring life dancer.

When I was a newly married young adult straight out of college, some of life's dance movements were riveting with consistent moving and relocation as a military family. The stage was regimented with stern rules and regulations and standing operating procedures (for both military and civilians and family members) that made one's life easier or a living hell. This dance stage could be lonely at the top; yet only the strongest and most determined dancer could move closer to the finale.

Dancing With Broken Bones reveals a combination of my personal life experiences, challenges and triumphs, ups and downs, victories and defeats. It chronicles the steps of an untrained dancer through many life experiences and presents various narratives on how the movements and the nuances of dance steps can serve as a therapeutic

14

route of escape and as a coping mechanism with life itself. I endeavor to share these personal life experiences through the lens of a dancer. I hope the stories will entertain, enlighten, or inspire you to embrace your own dance…. for such a time as this. Shall we dance?!

SECTION I

INTRODUCTION
TO THE DANCE

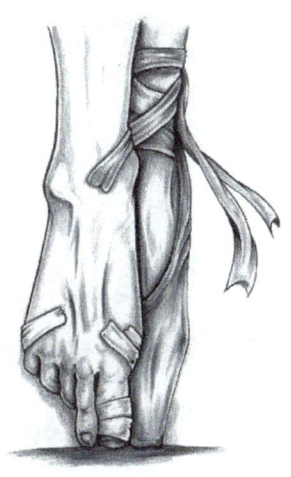

"Dance is the joy of movement and the heart of life."
~Author Unknown

Chapter One

"Baby Steps"

"To watch us dance is to hear our hearts speak."

-Indian Proverb

*O*nce upon a time of segregation in the magnolia State of Mississippi, in the Deep South in the 1950's, a very smart, talented and popular high school senior was preparing for her graduation. Being popular among your peers and teachers could have its benefits. Ethel Julia, but among her friends she was known as E.J., was Nia's mother and was all that and a bag 'o chips! Smart, intelligent, musically and academically astute. She was a majorette and played the flute in the marching band. She and her 'BFF' were voted 'most popular' in their senior high school class. Yet, she was a little bit too popular. E.J. was scheduled to graduate in May with the Class of 1954. E.J. found herself dancing the 'Twist' after she discovered she was pregnant in the beginning of her graduating year. E.J. and her father, Dave, were convinced she could still graduate on-time. As a result, E.J. concealed her pregnancy by tightly tying her stomach down during the first four or five months of her pregnancy. No one knew of her dance 'Twist' except her father. Her 'Twist' was a well-kept secret.

On October 14, 1954, E.J. had a little girl weighing in at a whopping 4 pounds 4 ounces. I don't know if incubators were available to provide additional care in 1954. But in the words of the late great James Brown, "papa's got a brand new bag....hey!" This baby's dance steps were about to begin. Nia entered life on an unusual dance stage. As a little girl who figuratively and ofttimes literally grew up in a "juke joint" (aka a café), Nia was constantly surrounded by music and dancing. In the Juke Joint, Nia experienced music hits from colored (African-American) artists like Nat King Cole, Chuck Berry, Muddy Waters, Fats Domino, Little Richard, James Brown, Aretha Franklin, Marvin Gaye, The Supremes and so many more.

E.J. graduated right on time with honors. But on her quiet stage, she was twisting all by herself. No confessed boyfriend or dance partner. E.J. was the only girl. She had three younger brothers. All four were one year apart. E.J.'s mother must have been a woman of many dance movements being with child four consecutive years. That dance deserves an encore: bravo, bravo madame.

Nia began to have questions about her own dance therapy. So, what happens when two people engage in a dance when neither person has a sense of good direction or movement? Who is leading? Who is following? Can there be a simultaneous mixture of movements? This literary dance performance shares the story of three siblings who were raised in the same household by two matriarchs. It should be noted that both matriarchs danced Nia's dance first! Two brothers and one sister were raised in the same household. Unfortunately, Nia's young innocent eyes witnessed boyfriends come and go in her mother's young adulthood. Nia was constantly reminded by her mother that the father's name on her birth certificate was not her 'real' daddy and one day Nia's mother said she would tell her who her 'real' daddy was.

Dancing with Broken Bones

When Nia was six years old, her mom birthed twin boys. All three were born in a local, Catholic hospital. Nia took great pride in being the "Big Sister" as she helped to attend to her little twin brothers through the years. To this day, Nia still has a copy of a picture from when she was about eight years old where the twin brothers, Larry and Harry, were seated in twin baby chairs in their front yard. Nia was standing in the middle with a switch in her hand. Supposedly the switch symbolized Nia's image of corporal control in their innocent and tender dance movements of childhood.

A touching yet heartbreaking change in this dance is when the mother led the dance, she consistently advised Nia that she would one day tell her who her real daddy was; yet the point was always noted from Nia's mother that the twin brothers' daddy was not her real daddy either.

Strong dance shoes were required for these static yet dynamic dance steps. The matriarchs for Nia and her twin brothers were entrepreneurs. Nia's family history suggests that her granddaddy's employer moved the family from Meridian to Vicksburg to Jackson, Mississippi between the 1930s and the 1960s. Sadly the dance of divorce hit the family in the mid 50's. Yet Nia's mother and grandmother had the backbone, strength, and determination to not go off-stage defeated. These strong women were going to dance this dance or die!

The matriarchs' family business, Ethel's Tea Room, was a restaurant by day and a juke-joint by night. Monday through Friday during the day full-course, hot lunches were served to the workers of Nia's granddaddy's workplace, Faulkner Concrete & Pipe Company. At

20

night Ethel's Tea Room transitioned into a juke joint. The juke joint was where Nia was introduced to her own private and public dance floor and to dances like the jerk and the "Watusi".

Some of Nia's favorite dance moves included the Boogaloo. The Boogaloo was danced to fast, upbeat music where there were lots of shoulder movements, hips moving up and down, circular rapid leg motion and smooth footwork. Chubby Checker's twist was one of the simplest of all dance styles; you can either do it standing or moving up and down. The juke-joint served as Nia's public and private dance academy. She could sneak in a practice while the Motorola was playing a fast dance tune before Ethel's Tea Room got busy with customers.

On the other hand, there were times when Ethel's Tea Room was crowded and in full-effect with customers dining in for lunch or dinner. Couples and singles seemed to release any worries, problems, frets or fears while dancing to their favorite rock-n-roll or blues artist on the dance floor. At nightfall, the atmosphere in the juke joint was strictly for lovers only. There was a lot of slow drags and bump-n-grind dance going on. This was quite the dance academy for Nia.

Since she started to walk, Nia always loved to move her little body to music. Her beloved granddaddy would be so tickled to see her wiggle her little limbs to the boogie-woogie beats coming from the jukebox. Popular dance moves back then included the "Boogaloo", "Twist", the "Locomotion", the "Mashed Potato", Rufus Thomas' "Funky Chicken", the "Hitch-hike", the "Jerk" and many others. Chubby Checker' 1959 song, "The Twist " catapulted the interest of Dick Clark on a popular television show, American Bandstand. The Locomotion, co-written by Carol King, was a modified line dance in which participants formed a single-file train that snaked through the dance floor.

At the age of seven, Nia and a neighbor kid (aka Domino) aged 10 or 11, competed in a local talent show that was held every Wednesday night at the Alamo Theatre in downtown Jackson, Mississippi. This weekly amateur talent night included people of all ages to showcase their talents of acting, singing, dancing, etc. To their great surprise and delight Domino and Nia won the talent show one Wednesday night. For Nia, this ignited an eternal love with the art form of dance. Nia's parents (a mother, grandmother and granddaddy) could not afford to send her to any formal dance classes back then in the segregated south (1950s and 1960s). As a result, Nia fulfilled her love of the dance by dancing in Ethel's Tea Room and in the living room to any television show that showcased dance…. any kind of dancing.

Through the years, Nia watched shows like American Bandstand and Soul Train. As an introvert, she found that dancing presented itself as therapeutic for whatever bothered or upset her as a means to get her through conflict or challenging times. Being immersed in dancing or watching others dance always brought Nia joy! In Nia's childhood, children were seen and not heard. It was disrespectful to engage in 'grown folks' (adult) conversations.

Until you reached the age of accountability, which in Nia's family's view, was eighteen years old. You spoke when you were spoken to or you would get your tail whipped with a switch, belt,

whatever your mama, big mama, or any adult could get their hands on.

For Nia, it was just so much better to speak through dancing.

Chapter Two

"Teen Swing"

"Dance is art; paint your dream and follow it."

-Steven Thompson

*N*ia experienced many dance movements in her childhood including the birth of her twin brothers in 1960. Nia was about to experience the quick steps of the samba or maybe the pasodoble as she was now a 'big sister' who was large and in-charge of the twins. Her mama and grandmother had to purchase twin doll babies, so Nia could imagine raising and attending to her own twins just like her mama! Oh, what an attentive big sister she was becoming at the age of six and seven. She was so good at watching the twins while her mom and grandmother were busy working in the juke joint late nights and every weekend.

Nia had to mature and grow up faster than her peers. Nia learned customer service in the Juke-Joint. Nia learned how to wash dishes, wait tables and take orders, and use a cash register. She could count money and make change just like her mom and her 'Badear'; her granddaddy whom she considered her dad and her best friend. You see, Nia has never really known 'who' her biological father is or was. She was given the name of the person who was / is listed on her birth certificate. Why was this dance a mystery? Nia didn't really let this mystery bother her because her granddaddy was the only daddy/father she would ever know. She met the man whose name was on her birth certificate maybe twice in her childhood; yet her mother reminded her innocent little self, that 'he' wasn't really her father and one day she would tell her who her daddy really was. Why was this dance such a mystery? Would this dance

25

ever be on center stage? Nia managed to allow the image and the person of her granddaddy be the only daddy she really needed to know. And her life's dances continued.

On a novice dance stage, Nia hated kindergarten because they seemingly served pork and beans every day. She complained so much about kindergarten making her sick, her mother and grandmother took her out of kindergarten. Yet she loved her elementary school. She attended her first two and half school years at the now 'historic' Smith Robertson Elementary School. Nia was about to enter her dance stage with a new dance: transition and relocation. This dance was fast and swift. Her childhood neighborhood was a vibrant and lively community called "Under the Hill." This long-gone community should have been declared a historical landmark in the City of Jackson, Mississippi.

Yet due to eminent domain the colored residents and business owners who lived and worked "Under the Hill" had to move in the mid 1960's. Nia and her family had to relocate to a new neighborhood on the north side of town. Nia had to change schools. This literal dance move was never forgotten. This was the era where corporal punishment (spanking or whipping with a switch or belt) was acceptable in the public school system. Nia adored her teachers in first and second grade. But her third-grade teacher was mean. If Nia did not listen to instruction, her third-grade teacher would hit her in the palm of her hand with a yardstick (ruler). Nia hated her and welcomed the opportunity to change schools and leave this dance partner far behind. Good riddance!

Her new school was within walking distance of her mother and grandmother's new home in the suburb (Virden Addition) where life seemingly would be so much better. Life became mo' better with a new dance.

As a little colored girl born in the Deep South in the mid 50's to a young 17-year-old mother, Nia entered the world with a dancing purpose. She was Nia because she was seen but not allowed to be heard. She was Nia because she wanted to dance with purpose and brilliance yet had no voice. The only person who was compassionate enough to hear Nia's voice was her granddaddy. Nia's granddaddy always had the time and the patience to…. listen to her voice and embrace each dance. Whether she talked about her fatigue from washing a lot of dishes in the café (aka Ethel's Tea Room) or talked about having to babysit and watch her little twin brothers as she was only a child herself. Nia had no voice. So, she danced!

Nia felt guilty and over-burdened at the same time as a little girl given responsibilities way beyond her years. Before Nia reached the age of 12, she could wash and dry dishes, sweep and mop floors, clear and wipe down tables, and assist customers at the "Juke Joint." She could operate a cash register and make change for patrons paying for home-cooked meals, snacks, sodas and beer. There was very little time to 'go outside and play' like her little playmates. Whenever she could escape from her work duties, her route of escape was either making mud pies under the house, or dancing in the yard, or dancing in the Juke Joint where her granddaddy would give her quarters to dance so others could see just how skilled and talented she was.

Nia could dance every dance that was popular in the late 50's and in the 60's (the jerk, boogaloo, mashed potatoes, etc.) Her dance moves made her granddaddy laugh out loud. She recalls hearing his robust voice saying, "Come on granddaughter, show 'em how you can roll yo' belly and dance!!!" The floor in the Juke Joint…. was her center stage for the dance. Dancing allowed her to get everybody's attention. Her dancing seemed to make people smile and be happy. Nia loved the attention on her little stage. But once the dance was over, life was back to its normal routine…. work, work, and more work.

Nia's granddaddy was always her 'knight-in-shining-armor' when she was afraid to ask her two lead dancers, Mama and Badear, for something special. Nia asked her granddaddy to ask her Mama and Badear if she could have a Sweet Sixteen birthday party. Her mama agreed and stipulated how many neighbor kids could attend and that she and her guests could even have a bottle of Boone's Farm wine. Honey hush yo' mouth! That dance was gon' be lit! Of course, the two bouncers at the party - were none other than her Mama and Badear. That was the #BESTBIRTHDAYEVER!!!

Junior High School was quite enjoyable and uneventful. Nia and her neighbors walked to and from school each day. Life's dance stage seemed good. Now Nia had emerged into her high school years. Another twisted tango turn evolved in the middle of Nia's 10th grade. After her class had made ALL plans for their high school graduation two years ahead of time, the State of Mississippi passed the desegregation law instituting mandatory desegregation of all public schools. Evidently, Nia was born to dance through joy….and pain; sunshine and rain. This mandatory desegregation split what would have been a happy Class of 1972 at Brinkley High School. Yet, it turned into a bitter and painfully integrated high school experience that is still a miserable memory 50 years later. Like a bad toothache with medication and extraction, the pain of this dance…. still lingers within the heart of each member of this graduating high school class. Words cannot even express the agony and emotional pain felt by all of Nia and her high school classmates in the 10th grade. Neighbor kids that you have played with, studied with, maybe even got in a little trouble with were now a split group; a split graduating class at two different high schools.

How could a mandatory state legislative policy bring so much mental and emotional pain to a group of teenagers who just wanted to successfully complete high school with the peers they have known since elementary school and move on with their productive adult lives? Oh Lord, why was this happening to us? Why now? This Teen Swing dance was in the words of songwriter Natalie Cole painful and "Unforgettable".

Fifty years later, Nia still feels the sting and the pain of that mandatory desegregation of her high school class that was divided in half when she and her classmates were forced to shift the dance to two different high schools. The emotional and mental pain of that academic dance separation is still evident in the New Millennial. Each ten-year class reunion is held on separate dance stages. Communications and relationships for the most part are still on separate dance stages. The bottom line is the former tenth grade class of Brinkley High School still suffers a P.T.S.D. of being forced to academically dance on a stage no one asked for. Maybe dancing separate and equal would have been better for a smooth dance stage. Yet Nia and all of her classmates have pushed forward through much prayer and supplication and learned no matter what… to just keep dancing!

Chapter Three

"Young Adult Dancer"

"I have no desire to prove anything by dancing...I just dance."

-Fred Astaire, Actor/Dancer

*G*raduating from an "integrated" high school led to so many mixed emotions. It was a pivotal moment in Nia's history as she transitioned from a teen to young adulthood. Nia's and her classmates' hearts were still in the hallways of their beloved Brinkley High School. They were born to be just like Brinkley High School's mascot: Eagles. Eagles are on the ground only when it's necessary. Their classmates' desire was to "fly baby fly!" Nia decided to follow in her mother's footsteps and attend Jackson State University. At dear ole Jackson State, Nia would find comfort and confirmation in a predominantly African American environment. During Nia's matriculation at Jackson State the student enrollment (1972-1976) was probably 98% Black: student body, instructors, coaches, and staff. Emotionally, maybe this would make up for Nia and her classmates' horrific and forced desegregation in the midst of high school.

Of course, attending college in one's hometown had its dancing ups and downs. Nia's little hooptie (a 15-year-old Dodge) was dying a slow, painful dance. Nia had been driving on the down low (especially at night) since she was 12 or 13 years old. When Nia received her driver's permit at 15, she drove all over her hometown running errands for her mother and grandmother. Taking the road test at DMV at the age of 16 was a piece of cake. God's grace had protected Nia from the womb…...for such times as these. Upon entering college, the Dodge hooptie was on its last dance. Enter Nia's granddaddy to center stage. There was no way Nia's granddaddy was going to allow Nia to ride a "bus" to college. Oh but No! Nia's granddaddy started networking. A local auto body shop had purchased a Toyota Corolla that had fallen off of a moving train and rebuilt the exterior car body. Fortunately, none of the mechanical parts were damaged. Granddaddy showed his best dance move through a Flex. A Flex dance symbolizes there's no position this dancer cannot do!

Nia initially chose Sociology as her college major. By the end of her Freshman year, her one philosophy class changed her mind. The instructor was talking about all kinds of strange mental and emotional disorders people experience. Nia meditated and pondered over how she had witnessed her mother and grandmother working tirelessly, yet so humbly, in Ethel's Tea Room (aka the juke joint) during her childhood neighborhood, "Under the Hill"! They seemed to enjoy catering to and serving people. People patronizing Ethel's Tea Room always seemed so happy to enjoy home-cooked lunches, not to mention the mesmerizing nuances of couples dancing through their 'bump-n-grind' motions at night, especially on the weekends, when the dance partners were different at night than they were in the daytime. Nia could not imagine choosing a profession where you have to deal with people's deep thoughts and emotions. Nia changed her mind and promptly switched her major to Business Administration. Nia's dream was to complete her bachelor's degree, then a Master of Business Administration (MBA), get a great-paying job, find a cute little bachelorette apartment and live happily ever after. Wrong dance!!!

Dancing with Broken Bones

Two life-changing events happened in Nia's sophomore and junior year at Jackson State. She met and dated a guy who had just pledged Alpha Phi Alpha who was absolutely smitten with her. He was so smitten that he and his fraternity brothers mentally harassed her in their shared Business Communications class because Nia would always be the first student to complete every written exam, turn in the exam to the instructor and exit the room. Her boyfriend and his frats were furious with her academic dance to say the least. While Nia spent the summer of 1974 in Detroit with her uncle, aunt, and their infant son, Nia's fraternity boyfriend wrote non-stop letters begging her to hurry and return to Mississippi. Nia wasn't all that attracted to the dude at the time but he was the kindest and most thoughtful young man she had allowed to get close to her heart.

Nia returned South in mid-August and was already on the pledge line with 31 other young collegiates with the Delta Pi Chapter, Delta Sigma Theta Sorority, Inc. Nia was Duck #17, "Sad Sack". The sorority's big sisters gave Nia this horrible line name because she was a 99-pound weakling and her pants used to sag in the butt all the time.

Once Nia successfully became a "Delta Girl," her boyfriend was in the ROTC Program and would be commissioned as a 2d Lieutenant in the U.S. Army upon graduation. Nia and her ROTC boyfriend became engaged, and a small ceremony was held in her granddaddy's living room on a Saturday afternoon in October 1975. Nia's step-grandmother worked as a domestic for a local white family. The step-grandmother borrowed a wedding dress from her employer for Nia.

Dancing with Broken Bones

Nia and her new husband, her sorority sisters, and his fraternity brothers and family celebrated at a local community center's club house. Nia was a young adult dancer about to launch off into a tumultuous tango with lots of lifts, exhilarating movements and brief stops to develop what would be memories of a lifetime. This dancer was about to take new strides on her dance floor as she was transitioning from a married college graduate to a young Army Officer's wife. Preparing to become a military wife did not come with an instruction manual or as they say in the military there was no SOP (Standing Operating Procedure) to give Nia any guidance on what she was about to experience. The only experience Nia had acquired was how to dance in a Juke Joint, how to dance through elementary, high school, and through a Historical Black College / University (HBCU) campus. Seems maturity, good manners, and common-sense would-be Nia's new dance book for her life-changing next chapter. Nia was about to become a Dancing U.S. Army Officer Wife! Let the new dance begin.

SECTION II

TANTELIZING TANGO

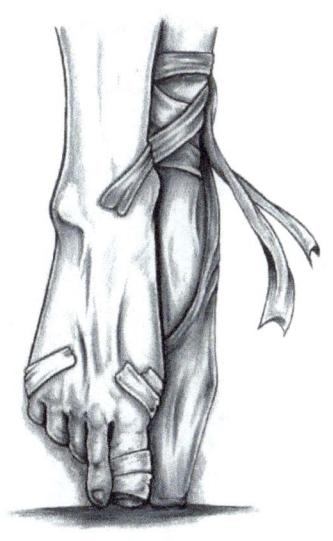

"You dance love, and you dance joy, and you dance dreams."

~Gene Kelly

Chapter Four

"Military Spouse Dancer"

"Learn the craft of knowing how to open your heart and to turn on your creativity. There's a light inside of you."

-Judith Jamison, American Dancer and Choreographer

*N*ia was entering a brand-new center stage as a U.S. Army Officer's wife. Her college sweetheart, now husband, was commissioned as a 2LT in the U.S. Army. Their first duty station was Fort Campbell, Kentucky where their first baby boy was born January 24, 1978, in the midst of a terrible ice and snowstorm. Not to mention Nia's birthing dance was via Lamaze technique. No pill! No epidural! Just a lot of heavy breathing and words that will curl a saint's hair. Will the creator and designer of 'le Lamaze' please report to center stage and be stoned! Nia is now on center stage as a military wife and new mother: lights, camera, and a lot of different kinds of dance action. To add fuel to this dance fire, Nia's military husband received 'permanent change in duty station orders' (PCS) orders to Korea, unaccompanied orders when their baby was only three-months old. This was about to become a solo performance.

All kinds of dance motions were on Nia's stage at this time. So much for her working 3 or 4 months on her first government job as a GS-02. Pregnant with extreme morning sickness for nine long months. Now her new husband of two and half years was leaving her with a new baby!

Her childhood Under the Hill, her transition from an all segregated to a desegregated high school environment to becoming the first grandchild on her maternal side of the family to graduate from college could have never prepared her for this transformative and unforgettable solo dance performance.

Would she put her best dance foot forward and succeed through rotating dances every three years and transferring with her spouse to new duty stations? With each new reassignment one had to take a bow from a familiar dance stage, the curtain falls, lights go off. Within a 30-60 day permanent change-of-station transition, you find yourself leaving behind acquaintances and coworkers and neighbors and ofttimes life-long friends. The familiar stage is left behind: new acquaintances and coworkers and neighbors and neighborhoods (on post or off post) greet you on a brand-new dance stage. The nuance of some dances may be the same (i.e., commissary, post exchange, troop medical and dental clinics, off post activities and entertainment, etc.); yet there is now a different stage, different audience.

The rhythm and dance of a military family is very unique. One must be open to constant dance motions and loads of swift transitions with rigid rules and regulations. One main dance step that family members and military/government civilians must learn to dance is the importance of honoring your country, your flag, your military and your identification card. Not learning the nuances of these dance steps will present swift, strict dance movements with or without penalties! The clarion call for this Army dance would be "hoo-aww!" Nia's dance would come with ease with her level of confidence on the military spouse dance floor. A grand salute to Nia's customer service dance training over 20 years ago in a theater "Under the Hill" lovingly described as a "Juke-Joint".

The dance experiences in Nia's grandmother's "Juke-Joint" provided good training ground for working with and for persons from different parts of the United States and the world. The first duty station at Fort Campbell, Kentucky was not too bad. It was only a seven- or eight-hour drive back to her beloved hometown, Jackson, to periodically visit family during holidays and special family occasions. This new "military spouse" dance encumbered Nia to become acquainted with the 'Officers' Wives Club" aka the "OWC." Nia's military spouse directly and gently as possible encouraged her on the importance of her visibility and importance of participating in the Officers' Wives Club. It was a silent, maybe not too silent, rule of military engagement that if a company grade (Lieutenant to Captain) officer wanted to be promoted and he or she was married, promotion would look more favorable "IF" the female spouse participated in the OWC. The decision for Nia to become an actively engaged member of the OWC was non-negotiable. Nia desired that her military husband received all the accolades, awards, promotions and any other added benefits to further his military career. Nia was likely the youngest wife in the club and was the only African-American wife in this particular OWC.

For the next 24 months, Nia attempted to be a stay-at-home Army wife. That did not work too well for a driven, college-educated, and independent Nia. After attending monthly OWC coffees with the wives and periodic volunteer activities at a thrift shop on post organizing and sorting and displaying gently used clothing, household goods, and other commodities, Nia convinced herself to either apply for a job or go crazy from absolute boredom. Her biggest excitement as a new Army wife was getting a cute little black and white puppy from a local pet shop that she and her husband named Scottie. Nia and her husband bought Scottie while they lived temporarily in a nicely furnished trailer home right across the highway from the Army installation. As they remained on the housing waiting list, Nia and her husband spent a lot of evenings and weekends with another young Army couple, Charles and Frances. Nia's husband and Charles were fraternity brothers. Charles was engaged to Frances at the time. Scottie was like the canine nephew who brought great joy to both couples.

In the summer of 1976, Nia, her husband, and Charles decided to drive to Nashville (about an hour's drive from the Army post) to do a movie and dinner. The weather forecast was for rain and thunderstorms later that evening. They could not have guessed how severe that storm would be. With their dog Scottie resting back at their cozy little trailer, this threesome noticed the weather rapidly changing with dark clouds and the rains becoming heavier and heavier. The closer they approached the Clarksville area, the weather worsened. The weather forecast on the radio was not good.

By the time Nia and her husband dropped Charles off at his BOQ (Bachelor Officers Quarters), the visibility was almost zero. Instead of staying with Charles in a brick building, Nia and her husband persisted in returning to the trailer to check on little Scottie. Wind gusts now must have been about 40 - 50mph. As they entered the property all kinds of debris was blowing in the wind. As they opened the front door of the trailer, the strong winds practically pulled the door off the hinges. There awaited a shaken and very nervous 'lil puppy in his cage. Upon picking Scottie up in an attempt to calm him down, Nia saw the walls of the trailer go in and out, in and out. She screamed and shouted, "We gotta get out of here before we die!" Her husband was trying to calm her down and insisting they keep safe by remaining in the trailer. Nia had to design a new dance entitled, "exit stage I'm outta here!" It was one of the most terrifying moments Nia had experienced as a young adult. There was no staying inside of that trailer with the walls going in and out, in and out. As Nia held Scottie in her arms approaching the door of the trailer to leave, Nia's husband screamed at her asking, "Where do you think you are going?" Nia was leaving with or without her husband.

Without further discussion Nia, her husband and little Scottie were in the car headed back to the post in an attempt to get inside of their friend's room at the BOQ for more safety. That solution worked. The storm passed over around midnight. Nia and her husband and Scottie returned to what would look like a war zone. The winds had disintegrated about every three or four trailers in this mobile home park. To this day Nia has a phobia of high wind gusts. Within the next month, Nia and her husband received a call that government quarters were available for them to move into on post. That was the best news ever!

After Nia and her husband and Scottie were settled into their first government quarters on post, Nia was becoming bored of being a "puppy mom" with nothing to do. So, she applied for a civil service position on post as a GS-02. At this point it wasn't about the money, it was about Nia's sanity and about making good use of all the money that her mother and grandmother had invested in her receiving a full college education debt-free without any student loans. Praise God from whom all blessings flow. Now that is enough right there and right here for a praise dance. For when praises go up; blessings come down. But God still had other plans. Around March/April 1977, Nia was pregnant and experiencing serious morning sickness. The sickness was so bad that Nia had to resign from her first civil service position.

Two life-changing events happened in January 1978: Nia's first baby son was born in the U.S. Army Hospital at Fort Campbell, Kentuc ky and her husband received relocation orders for a 12-month, unaccompanied assignment to Korea. With a newborn baby, they made the decision to put all their household goods in long term storage. Scottie had become very jealous of the baby and destroyed everything that smelled like the baby. Nia, little Trae and Scottie would return temporarily to her hometown to live with her mother, grandmother, and her twin brothers. Plus, Nia and her husband had recently bought a brand new 1978 Cutlass Supreme Brougham. Goodness that was the prettiest car she had ever seen (crimson and cream, her sorority colors). She was returning to her comfort zone with a new baby and a new car. Life was really good.

But storms come and storms go. In January 1979, Nia had planned a one-year birthday party for her little baby boy and the day before the birthday party on January 23rd, Nia's beloved granddaddy died in his sleep. How does one go from a fast rhythmic cha-cha to a stepper, a dancer who makes the most elegant moves full of grace and style? Even when no one is watching, Nia's life dance movement was starting to present as a Cheerleader cheering everyone on in her dance arena to 'That Dancing Girl' a dancer who seems to never take a break.

After Nia's military husband returned from his one-year duty in Taegu, Korea a new dance was about to begin. A new stage, a new city, a new dance. The next duty station (1980-1982) was at Fort Gordon, Georgia. Nia had a young toddler with a lot of energy. Nia just could not fathom staying home dancing through their government quarters 24/7. This was going to take a supernatural move of almighty God to come to her rescue. A homemaker and stay-at-home-mom, Nia was not!

God showed up once again. Nia applied for another Civil Service job and when her first baby turned two, one of the Warrant Officers assigned in Nia's husband's unit shared that his wife was a home daycare provider and had space for one more. Bless the Lord for "Ms. Pat". Ms. Pat had two school-aged children of her own but ended up providing home daycare for four little boys: three Caucasian and Nia's little boy - African American. This dance was about to become inviting and invigorating, to say the least.

The assignment at Fort Gordon, Georgia contained various dance routines for Nia. Nia's spouse went away on TDY (Temporary Duty) assignments as he was progressing in rank from Lieutenant to Captain. These various promotions encumbered her husband with long hours and lots of unaccompanied duty travel. Nia had to find innovative ways to keep herself occupied to negate boredom. As a result, she worked a short-term Civil Service position (GS-04), Secretary. Once that temporary appointment ended, Nia needed something to get out of the house a few hours per week and decided to work in retail at a local mall in Augusta, Georgia. Of all places, she was hired as a part-time clerk at Spencer Gifts. The retail gift items in this store ranged from nice to absolute naughty! The dance repertoire of giftings could be described as everything from general special occasion birthday cards to vibrators that resembled body parts. For the sake of the general reader, let's just keep it at that!

In 1982, a new dance was about to begin as permanent change of service (PCS) orders were received once again. This time, Nia and her military spouse and young son were headed to Augsburg, Germany. Nia and her family had to say Auf Wiedersehen (goodbye) to Ms. Pat and say Guten Tag (hello) to the new dance stage. Not only did Nia and her young son have to endure several immunizations prior to departure from the United States, but no one prepared Nia for the dance of culture shock. It was bad enough to say goodbye to both her family and her husband's family to go on a journey so very far away. How does one dance over an ocean hundreds of miles away and get a standing ovation? This was going to be a dance journey of a lifetime.

It took Nia about six months to get over or get through the culture shock. Everything - absolutely every dance number was different. Nia had to get another driver's license enabling her to drive in

Germany both on base (Kaserne), out on the economy (local village/town) but especially out on the Autobahn (the super-highway with no speed limit)! What in the world? Oh but Nia found a daycare center for little Trae; secured a full-time civil service job as a Secretary/Office Automation at a military Troop Medical Clinic (TMC) on one of the Kaserne's (bases) and discovered that her sorority had a chapter in Germany. What??!! Ahh this was a time to put on some new dance shoes and shake a grove thang.... yea yea.

With one year under her belt in Germany, she was dancing and grooving on the job, learning to shop by herself out on the German economy, received her family member driver's license as she learned to read and recognize the German street signs in order to drive herself to different towns in Germany each month to sorority meetings alone or with her sorority sisters. The third weekend - all the husbands and significant others knew - don't make any plans at all on the third weekend of the month. That was strictly.... Delta weekend. Ahh we shonuff dancing now. Driving a little 300-series BMW through German villages and on the autobahn with no speed limit. Zoom Zoom was Nia's newest dance. This unique military dance stage was full of emotions.

Nia danced the birthing dance with her second bouncing baby boy in November 1986 while her family was stationed at Fort Lee, Virginia. Nia called this little bundle of joy her "afro baby" because he exited her womb with a thick head of hair with very strong lungs. Anthony, as we lovingly called him Ant-Ant, arrived as our second military brat!

Nia had become thoroughly acclimated to stepping up on a new dance stage about every three years without her vote or her permission. The United States Army had full rights and privileges as to when and where Nia and her family's next dance stage would be. From 1975 to her military spouse's retirement in 1995 the dance locations included: Fort Campbell, Kentucky; (an unaccompanied tour-of-duty to Korea for Nia's husband); Fort Gordon, Georgia; Augsburg, Germany; Fort Lee, Virginia; Kaiserslautern Germany; and last tour of duty and retiring at Fort Monroe, Virginia. Wow…. what an immense stage of work, travel, friendships, hidden relationships, new cultural experiences, and work experiences too numerous to write.

If Nia could change anything about this 20+ years of travel, hardship and transitions, it would be to ensure honesty and transparency would be the premiere ballerina on each and every stage. The dance stage of secrecy and infidelity absolutely murdered Nia and her military spouse's marriage. To be perfectly honest, guilt rested on both of their laps. As some would sadly say in retrospect, 'it is what it is!' Shall we move on to the next dance experience.

Chapter Five

"Dance of Divorce"

"Dance of divorce...a waltz of loss and emptiness that never ends!"

*R*ight about the 20-year anniversary of Nia's marriage…the ugliness of infidelity, lack of attention to the marriage, no date nights, less and less intimacy……this waltz is becoming a longer and longer dance number. On Super Bowl night 1998, Nia had been out and about most of the afternoon trying to make herself busy and distracted due to no peace, no love, no anything at home with her military spouse. Her spirit had become so restless to the point of numbness wreaking havoc in her very soul.

As she entered the front door of her home, she could hear her husband speaking on the phone upstairs. As she slowly climbed the stairs on her way to the master bedroom, she overheard her husband say to the caller, ".... baby next time I come to Atlanta you gotta make more time for us. I need more time with you, okay?!"

At this point Nia is standing midway of the stairway. As her husband is pacing back and forth, he suddenly realizes that Nia is standing on the stairs listening. He hurriedly releases the call and attempts to NOT be surprised. In his attempt to change the conversation and the horrific mood in the air, Nia asked, "So who was that on the phone that you want to spend more time with?" Her husband was choking on his words and only babbling came out of his mouth. Nia, with supernatural calmness said to him: "I tell you what, you go and

enjoy the Superbowl Game. When the game is over, we need to talk!"
Nia's husband looked stunned, embarrassed, and spooked, all at the
same time. Her husband repeatedly tried to reach for body contact. Nia
absolutely refused and said to him, "No, no, go and enjoy your game.
But you better believe we are going to talk when the game is over!" At
this point, Nia closed the bedroom door and retreated to the master
bedroom in total horror. She prayed and talked to God for a while as she
rehearsed how she would engage in what would be a gut-wrenching
conversation.

When the game ended, Nia was in bed with a lamp on. Her
husband turned the lamp off and climbed on his side of the bed and had
the audacity to attempt to snuggle next to her. That's when the ceiling
came off in that bedroom. Nia, sat up in the bed, turned the lamp back on
and asked, "So who was that on the phone?" He replied after moments
of stammering and stuttering, "Umm that was my uh, my uh…." Nia
said, "well you might as well spit it out. Who was that?" He replied, "my
daughter's mother!" What???

Through the years, the devil and distraction tapped on each dance
partner's shoulders. Divorce entered their dance floor. Nia's Twin
brother #1 (six years younger than the sister) attended college and
completed all but maybe nine credit hours until degree completion. Twin
#1 is a sharp, very intense and focused problem-solver and go-getter in
everything he does. Nia's mother and grandmother could always look to
Twin brother #1 to get a task accomplished and accomplished well.
Twin brother #1 simultaneously engaged 30 years in military reserve

service and worked for the government in the field of finance and accounting. He married and this union produced one son and one daughter. On or about the 20-year mark, Larry, Twin Brother #1, seemingly approached the same dance floor. Divorce entered his dance floor.

Harry, Nia's Twin brother #2 - same family, same blood, similar discipline, similar lifestyle, similar dance floor, but totally different dance steps. Life happened. Twin brother #2 was somewhat different in not only his physique but different in his persona and path of his life's journey. Twin brother #2 married as a young adult. His bride brought a very young daughter onto their dance floor.

Due to a segregated South in the 50's and 60s, both twin brothers had the opportunity as young teens (14 yr. old) to work as bus boys in a local, private and segregated country club. In spite of the nuance of separatism and segregation present on this dance floor, both brothers managed to learn and develop discipline and a strong work ethic especially when it came to meal preparation and customer service. Twin Brother #2 and his wife birthed two more daughters. Life seemingly had its ups and downs for Nia and her twin brothers. Twin #2 Divorced and entered his dance floor.

For forty plus years, these siblings had the opportunity to visit in person during brief family visits…and at a point during the 40-year journey, several family elders (mother, grandmother, grandfather, and uncles) all died.

Yet a common dance for all three siblings was divorce. Divorce is not a physical death; but it has been a gut-wrenching, heart-breaking and emotional experience that tends to present itself as a "waltz of loss and emptiness" that slows down and subsides: yet the movement never ends.

Chapter Six

"Da Transition Slide"

Dancing With the Enemy!

*J*anuary 1, 2007. Happy New Year Jesus! As Nia sat and listened to track #6 on the "Gospel Goes Classical" CD by Juanita Bynum and Jonathan Butler, the song "I Don't Mind Waiting on The Lord" truly ministered to her that evening after 8:30pm. Is this really a "Happy" New Year!? As much hurt as she's felt (experienced) in this nightmare relationship, Nia felt like King David did where this is now a time where she has to encourage herself. Lord Jesus!

What happened to that seemingly "fairy-tale" relationship some four years ago with a man she met in church one Sunday morning in 2002? Seemingly he showed up out of the blue? Was it random or planned? In retrospect, he (the visitor) did know a married couple in this newly planted congregation come to think of it! Did the couple tell this visitor there was an eligible woman in their congregation…? A woman who was divorced with a stable job, a home, a car, educated and attractive (okay that's what some have said about her)? Was it all a set-up? Or was this fate gone bad? Was this going to be a beautiful waltz full of grace and beauty? Or was it going to be a fast tango with lots of change, quick steps, toss and terrible turns? What was he looking for? A good wife? A companion? A First Lady? Another preacher's wife? What?

This torrential tango happened much too fast. A whirlwind dating all of maybe six months with all the magic and icing on the cake that almost any girl could ask for. Nia now believed it was too good to be true. June 1, they were married in a private ceremony with only their pastor, pastor's wife and two witnesses. Nia was sucked in when she was most vulnerable. She was longing to have "her own" man of God. Bad mistake. And since she didn't wait on the Lord, she has been suffering the consequences since then. Big stumble in her dance partnership! A week after their first-year anniversary (June 2003), supposedly wife #2 called their (Nia's) home looking for her final divorce decree from "Nia's" supposedly husband. That shocker almost took Nia out of here. Nia was in such emotional shock, she left "her" home and drove to her adopted work-dad's home.

Her testimony is that she did not even remember being behind the wheel of a car that horrific evening; nor does she recall how she mechanically was transported from point A to point B! The shock of it all. How can you be married to two spouses at the same time...legally??? Such deception! Such lies! Secrets killed her first marriage now here we go again --- lies, secrets, and deception again. Nia asked herself, "Why me Lord? Why me?" This was like dancing "The Saboteur" because they're always sabotaging other dancers on the dance floor! So, if he lied and concealed a legal relationship what else will he lie about? These supposedly weekend moving jobs? Who is he moving? Is he really moving somebody or is he demonstrating a sexual healing salsa with a woman somewhere else?

Well, there ain't no action in 'this' bedroom so somebody (woman? Man?) is hitting it somewhere. Why is it that anytime they were intimate, Nia notices a vaginal odor and discharge --- and when trying to get an explanation from him, he's dumb-founded and puzzled! 'Give me a freaking break," she exclaimed! Nia asked him to go seek medical attention because he's intimately sharing whatever is going on in his body with her body. So, until he's mature enough to seek medical help/treatment, no nookie from that cookie. This Girl doesn't want no Sugar Toots Dancer!!!

Nia seemed to have had more questions than answers about her sabotaged relationship! How or why would you desire to lead a flock of God's people as the Shepherd? Why is it that this supposedly man of God would take "potshots" at her before God's people in the sanctuary? Can he really be "that" insensitive? Does he not realize how he's hurting her ...emotionally? How can a person be so "holy" and live in such a religious box that they seclude themselves from the real world; they exclude themselves from the ones who loved them? It hurts so bad. The relationship had changed for the worse. Does he not see that? Nia hasn't experienced or felt joy and happiness with this dance partner in such a long time that her emotions towards him and their relationship had become numb! Even when he had the audacity to take her to a 5-Star restaurant for dinner they both sat and dined in a spirit of silence. The lively dancing has come to a screeching halt. Where was the joy? Neither of them enjoyed the conversation anymore. All he wanted to talk about...was the church. All he seemed to care about...was the church! What about us? Does he really see that everything is NOT all well at home? What happened to the so-called 'happy dancing'?

Dancing with Broken Bones

How can you portray yourself as a spiritual leader over a flock of God's people when your own house is falling apart from neglect and lack of attention? Don't clean or attend to the car anymore. Don't have time to assist with household upkeep and repairs! What about the bills! No conversation! No time together! No touching! No intimacy! No sharing! No belonging! Nothing!

It's all dead….as a door nail! Time has come for Nia to plan to work and work the plan! How can a significant other NOT buy anything for his sweetheart? It is such a hurtful thing to not have anything to open, not even an envelope, on Christmas morning. Receiving money to pay a bill weeks after Christmas Day is just not the same thing as receiving and opening some kind of gift on Christmas morning.

To make this horrific dance tango even worse, Nia recalls spending her last $100 to get this man something for Christmas. He opened the gifts and left them on the floor for two days before he put them away. He left an expensive men's fragrance set on the doggone dance floor. He eventually put it on top of his wardrobe. Nia felt totally humiliated ~ this is such a spirit of torment and she wanted out so she can get her joy back. She heard a songwriter say, "I can do bad all by myself!" Nia knew his initial "presentation" was too good to be true.

Why did she allow this dance partner to rush her to the dance floor in the first place? Had she become a restless dancer? Why did she accept his proposal for a dance of eternal endearment also known as marriage? What kind of brain fart had she experienced? Questions yet no answers. This was about to be a solo dance performance. Nia's upcoming New Year's Dance Resolution: "Single and Saved!" Nia danced through the planning and presenting of a powerful weekend ministry: "Kingdom Daughters Ministries: Stepping Out Into Divine Authority." The Holy Dance…..has now begun!

SECTION III

FREESTYLE

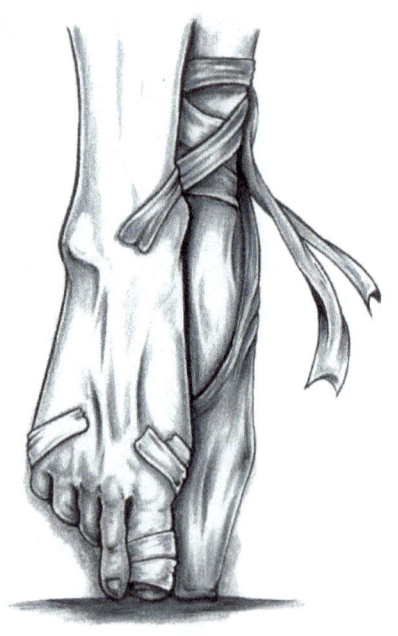

"Life isn't about waiting for the storm to pass ... it's about learning to dance in the rain."

-Vivian Greene

Chapter Seven

"Dancing with Wisdom"

"Every day brings a chance for you to draw in a breath, kick off your shoes, and dance."

— Oprah Winfrey

*T*he Lord began to put seasoned women in Nia's path. These seasoned women ranged in ages 50 to 93. In January 2010, Nia met a 93-year-old white female who was doing her grocery shopping in a local grocery store. As Nia offered to unload her grocery cart at the check-out counter, she attempted to decline the offer, but Nia persuaded her to accept help. As they talked in line, Nia asked if anybody was driving her home. The woman proudly explained that she still drives herself wherever she needs to go. Ninety-three years old and still driving. OMG! Nia noticed she had a six pack of Michelob Lite in her cart. Wanted to ask her "why" she was drinking or buying beer but figured at the age of 93 she had a right to her own choice of food and beverages. Her secret to longevity: Nia failed to ask her, but a viable suggestion would likely be that living a free and independent lifestyle has greatly enhanced her peace and longevity. Keep dancing momma, keep right on dancing!

Another dancing with wisdom encounter occurred in February 2010. Nia met a lady at the repast of a Homegoing Celebration for one of her sorority sisters and she shared with Nia that she was 92 years old. Nia exclaimed, "Wow – I would have never guessed it!" This senior beauty was immaculately dressed, her hair was perfectly coiffed with tasteful jewelry and other matching accessories. This woman was an absolute model and example of how a woman should present herself to others in public. This mature queen's presence exuded testimonies of dancing through life with wisdom. It was Nia's honor to sit at the feet with one who has pleasantly embraced longevity of life! Her life lesson to Nia was: "Don't worry about anything!" Yet her unspoken voice uttered to Nia's heart, "Just keep on dancing daughter! Keep right on dancing."

In the Holy Bible, King Lemuel wrote words his mother taught him regarding how to recognize a proverbial woman. The characteristics presented by this King in the Book of Proverbs of a "worthy woman" includes that she is "an excellent woman (one who is spiritual, capable, intelligent, and virtuous) ..." He further describes her as a woman who "equips herself with strength (spiritual, mental, and physical fitness for her God-given task).

Nia reflects her good fortune of having been among many "worthy women" who danced through life with wisdom, including her mother and grandmother. Nia's mother and grandmother made the word multitasking a household landmark. Neither allowed the dancing demon of divorce to hold them back. These two feminine powerhouses combined skills, abilities, persistence, passion and common sense as their blueprint for dancing with wisdom. They danced with many broken bones through motherhood, entrepreneurship, property management, and community advocate all together and made it look easy. As King Lemuel says.... "Many daughters have done nobly, and well (with the strength of character that is steadfast in goodness), but you excel them all. (Proverbs

31:29 AMP) "Give her of the product of her hands, and let her own works praise her in the gates (of the city.)" (Proverbs 31:31 AMP)

Nia experienced and encountered these kinds of phenomenal women all dancing with wisdom and broken bones throughout Nia's early childhood, teen years, young adulthood, and even into her mature adulthood. There was a dear friend of Nia's grandmother that her family lovingly knew as "Aunt Dood." Aunt Dood was a domestic worker for a white family in "da Sip," also known as Mississippi. Aunt Dood's domestic job description included attending to the needs of their white children, cleaning the home in an affluent, all white suburban neighborhood, cooking their meals and shining their floors. Her pay was likely very minimal. Yet her bonus was the ability to bring home extra food 'she' had cooked as she accepted hand-me-down children and adult clothing and shoes that the white family no longer wanted. Aunt Dood loved Nia and her two brothers like they were her own grandchildren. Aunt Dood's wise dance moves were not only working as a 'colored domestic worker', but she also lovingly attended to her father, Mr. Jim. Mr. Jim had some kind of long-term illness and was totally blind. In this new millennium his disease would likely equate to cancer. Aunt Dood may have been dancing with broken bones through her white family's domestic requirements but there were NO broken steps when she baked those homemade 'tea cakes' (honey huss yo' mouth) and chocolate cakes. That was a baking dance to last forever!

Nia's grandmother, Badear, only had a third-grade education. Badear danced with such great wisdom. She was wise enough, strong enough, and patient enough to handle her business and family matters. Badear's mentors must have been the Father, the Son, and the Holy Spirit. There's an ole saying, "the fruit don't fall (dance) too far from the tree!" Nia's mother found herself pregnant at the age of sixteen in her senior year in high school. Yet becoming an unwed mother didn't stop her from dancing. Matter of fact this situation must have compelled Nia's mother to PUSH: Pray Until Something Happens! Nia's young mother was determined to dance through the struggles and hard-knocks of her life. This young, determined Negro woman had multiple dance moves. Nia's mother watched her own divorced mother operate and manage a restaurant by day as it transformed to a "Juke Joint" by night. In the "Juke Joint" the people danced fast, high energy dance moves. Nia's mother and grandmother danced with wisdom as they likely prayed for their home situated next door to the Juke Joint. These two women were talented or blessed enough to be in the midst of multi-dance movements as they navigated the purchase of a new home in 1955 in a newly developed, all-colored neighborhood, Virden Addition, on the north side of the city.

Dancing with wisdom requires stamina and skills. Once the State of Mississippi and/or the City of Jackson, Mississippi instituted eminent domain on all personal properties of home/business owners located "Under the Hill," all the Colored/Negro businesses and homeowners were uprooted with swift dance movements from their places of comfort and stability. Yet, they kept right on dancing.

Life goes on. The Holy Bible declares, "He who has begun a good work in you will complete it until the day of Jesus Christ." (Philippians 1:6 NKJV) Through the years these women and so many more learned powerful life lessons: When you are served a bunch of lemons, squeeze and make some sweet lemonade. Above all things.... keep dancing!

Chapter Eight

"The Clinical Dance Academy"

"All the world's a stage, so dance on it."

"Sometimes in life confusion tends to arise and only dialogue of dance seems to make sense."

— **Shah Asad Rizvi**

*W*hen Nia was in the third grade, her mother, grandmother, and her twin brothers were moved from "Under the Hill" to a new suburb, Virden Addition in the same hometown. During this transitional dance Nia met her lifelong best friend forever (BFF) her "ride-or-die" girl, Serenity. Nia's clinical dance academy was about to begin. Nia's granddaddy had already set this particular dance stage as he would take Nia with him many Sundays after church service to have dinner with and visit various church member out in the countryside. Nia vividly recalls there was always so much home-made food at these homes. The aromas would meet you in the front yards as you pulled up to the home. These home visits were an absolute "set-up" for Nia's future in ministry. Her granddaddy was not a pastor, preacher, deacon, or church leader. Yet, her granddaddy profoundly did the work of ministry. Nia would see her granddaddy consistently leave the dining table and slip away to a nearby bedroom where there seemed to always be someone in the bed who appeared to be really sick and immobile. Nia's granddaddy would kneel down beside the person's bed and pray. This image would be an everlasting benediction to her granddaddy's own ministry. In today's vernacular it's known as pastoral care.

Around the fifth or sixth grade, Serenity convinced Nia to go and serve as volunteer candy-strippers at a local Jackson hospital. Serenity was always so excited to be in that clinical setting. For Nia just the thought of being around people wearing white uniforms and carrying syringes and connecting IVs in people's arms were not the dance moves for her. The bookmobile and the candy-striped uniform would serve as the first act on the stage that would touch the adult lives of Nia and Serenity yet in two different ways.

After completing high school, Serenity decided she would pursue the field of nursing. While Nia was persuaded, she would pursue a degree in business administration just like her mother. After both girls completed their respective degrees at two different local colleges, they both married in their early twenties. They both had two sons about the same ages. Their dance academies launched both Nia and Serenity to attend to and care for God's people but on two different stages: Serenity's stage was clinical as a NICU Nurse Case Manager and Clinician, while Nia initially worked in the business field with the U.S. Government in Civil Service.

Yet, after some 20 to 25 years, Nia's Dance Academy took a 360-degree pivotal turn from the business realm to the spiritual realm. 1998 - 2000 proved to be two years from hell for Nia. Nia experienced sudden death of her mother; change of career from government to private sector; separation and divorce; empty nest as her elder son left home for active-duty military and learning how to be a single woman for the first time in her adulthood. "All the world's a stage, so dance on it."

During the next fifteen years, Nia accepted her call to ministry, was licensed and ordained in the Gospel Ministry. And if that wasn't enough on her center stage, Nia completed a Master of Divinity (2010) and a Doctor of Ministry Degree (2014).

It was appearing that Nia and Serenity's clinical dance stages were now parallel to each other. Nia accepted the fact that God had a divine plan for her life. She found sweeter rest by trusting that God knew exactly what he was doing. Out of obedience, Nia yielded to the Holy Spirit and was attentive to divine direction. Nia worked full-time for local law enforcement and attended seminary. After completing her Master of Divinity, Nia enrolled and was accepted into a 12-month Chaplain Internship at a local hospital. She then applied for and was accepted into a 12-month Chaplain Residency at a different hospital in March 2017.

At this point, Nia felt prepared and ready to work as a professional clinical or pastoral counselor. April 2017, she applied for and began working as a PRN Hospice Chaplain, working 35-40 hours a week within a 50-mile radius. This position included being on-call some weeknights as well as weekends accumulating miles and wear and tear on her car, but especially on her body. The company's executive director repeatedly promised to make her a full-time employee with benefits. Nia kept praying and waiting for that promise to be fulfilled. After nine months of working and waiting, her patience grew short as she felt it was time to dance on a different stage.

Life has a way of transitioning us to a different dance stage.
Nia's former executive manager in the banking and law enforcement
industry and Nia's self-appointed mentor and life coach, Ridea
Richardson, wrote an inspiring book "Just Quit & Live: 367 Stories &
Meditations About Work, Monday's & Hope." Richardson wrote "if you
want to 'Just Quit' your job: you are not alone and you are not crazy."
She further shared "I wrote this book so people will KNOW that they are
not alone, and they are not crazy. There are thousands of others who are
miserable in their jobs and feel the need to "Just Quit." So, on the
morning of Monday, December 25 (Christmas Day), Nia woke up and
decided this was her last week with this hospice company. Nia
completed all patients' visits for the remainder of the month. Her last
dance on that job was Friday, December 29, 2017. Her proclamation
was: "I Quit!"

Chapter Nine

"The Bump and Grind"

"Dancing with the feet is one thing, but dancing with the heart is another."

- **Author Unknown**

Nia spent the first few months of 2018 attempting to find herself again. What would be her new dance routine? Would she require a dance partner, or would this be another solo performance? Nia began to recall the myriad dance stages of her life. From the boogaloo to the wytootsie to the jerk and even the freestyle, Nia had danced for so long and with so many partners on so many stages both near and far, which dance was waiting in the wings? After much prayer and meditation and seeking counsel from a very few trusted colleagues, Nia felt it was time she put all of her multiplicity of dance routines (good, bad, and the ugly) to work in her favor.

This creation would likely include the kinds of stages and partners from her past, even times she performed in a solo performance. As a former military spouse, prior government employee with the U.S. Civil Service, a myriad of employment from retail, non-profit, banking, sales, clinical, law enforcement, to congregational ministry. Were all of these dance movements for naught? Why on earth would someone with a myriad of dance experiences, all this education (Bachelor, Master Degrees and a Doctorate) continue to work for someone else? What kind of new dance movement could possibly be left?

Well Nia decided she would step out on faith and put her Doctor of Ministry and her dual board-certifications as Pastoral Counselor and Clinical Chaplain on a brand-new dance stage named: Ventura Consulting Group LLC. As a result, Ventura was born in May 2018.

This would be Nia's brand-new dance stage to provide pastoral care and counseling to those who needed attending to with tender loving care. No one warned Nia that dancing on a stage with no support on your feet, no dance partner to help balance the unexpected whirls and twirls that may result in falling flat on your face. At the beginning of this Ventura dance, Nia had a huge heart and big expectations of helping people address and work through varied conflicts and challenges in their personal lives. This stage required much more research and preparation than Nia had envisioned. Preparations that should have transpired included coaching from a wise business advisor, available and ready finances, business space/location, furnishings, office equipment, etc. Finances was the premiere spotlight on this stage event. Nia was blessed to find a structure close to her home where entrepreneurs, novice and established, could rent spaces for their business on a month-to-month basis with 24-hour access to include choice of three different meeting rooms, a kiosk with tables/chairs, refrigerator/freezer, sink and other basic amenities to host your client/customer. It seemed a perfect fit. Yet without start-up capital and no financial plan, it was a dance of disaster waiting to happen.

Nia had one primary cheerleader and several angels. These angels arranged and presented the best business launch/open house ever.

It all started out well. Yet Nia's clients were few and far between. This dancer limped onto the entrepreneurial stage long enough to fulfill the one-year rental contract. It was boom or bust! May 2019 this dance unfortunately ended with a sad curtain call.

In spite of apparent chronic burnout and a great need to rest from all of life's dancing, on April 27, 2019, Nia began a brand-new dance season by packing up and moving down south to her beloved Mississippi. Nia returned to where it all began. For the first 30 days of transition, Nia found herself dancing through change/transition, culture shock, grief and mourning. Nia was on center stage going through the "medium of dance" best explained by Paige Arden as 'dance not being something that can be explained in words....it has to be danced." She found herself emotionally as the 'cumbersome gawker,' a dancer who has no idea how to coordinate themselves.

Nia had entered a season as "Calamity Jane," a calamity waiting to happen! The temptation to turn around or return to a place of comfort and familiarity was overwhelming. The only place of familiarity and solace was the role of a chaplain, either law enforcement or clinical - her 'happy places.' Her happy places were places where she could dance (work) with happy feet. She longed for the Dance of Grace where her movements were easy and stress-free. As long as Nia remained within the boundaries of dignity, respect, and proper protocol, this dance was soothing to her soul; a dance she could engage in for hours and hours without remembering to take a break for fatigue was not even in the atmosphere. Time for a 'Dance of Intermission'.

This Dance of Grace was manifested through her twice a week visits as a Volunteer Chaplain where it all began: the St. Dominic's Hospital. Isn't it amazing how God can bring us one full circle? Nia and Serenity started as youthful, volunteer candy-strippers at the University Hospital as pre-teens. Now Nia, a mature, experienced and board-certified clinical chaplain and pastoral counselor found herself right back on the stage where it 'literally' all began at St. Dominic's Hospital.

SECTION IV

CENTER STAGE/SOLO PERFORMANCE

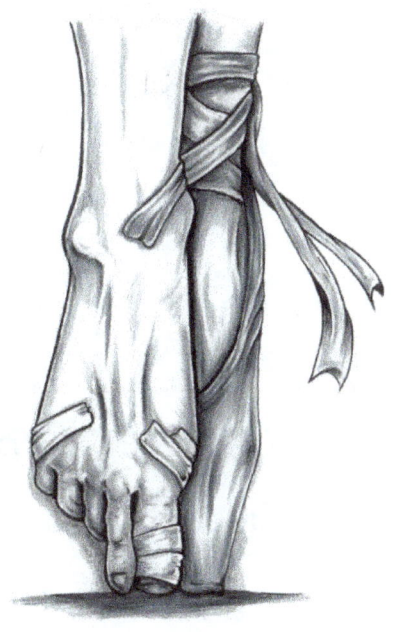

"Great dancers are not great because of their technique, they are great because of their passion."

~Martha Graham

Chapter Ten

"My Gift is My Dance"

"Reputation is what men and women think of us;

character is what God and angels know of us."

-Thomas Paine

*H*ow in the world do you return to your birthplace after some 50+ years? Christmas vacation in 2014, Nia was driving on Interstate 55 North returning to one of her brothers' homes after leaving a dinner in downtown Jackson after dining with several of her high school / college classmates. Nia passed by the large campus of the St. Dominic's Hospital. St. Dominic's was where Nia's dance started in October 1954. But here she was: daughter, woman, mother, sister, auntie, classmate, entrepreneur, preacher, teacher, board-certified counselor and chaplain, confidante and friend. Oh, what an unforgettable life dance. In the quietness of the drive, Nia thought to herself, how awesome it would be to one day return to work as a clinical chaplain at the hospital where she was born. It was a dream…. a fleeting dance nuance she thought would never happen.

As life would have it, the summer of 2019, Nia arrived at St. Dominic's Hospital about 8:15a.m. one weekday morning. She sat quietly in her car meditating before reporting for duty as a volunteer in the Pastoral Care Department. At 8:25a.m., she left her car as she felt she needed, in particular, to find the 'right' two vehicles to walk between in order to get onto the sidewalk, same sidewalk she had used for the last four weeks.

Dancing with Broken Bones

As Nia approached the sidewalk, she saw a woman seemingly in her early 70's carrying a purse on her right arm with a coffee thermos and two filled canvas bags hanging from her left arm. Nia said, "Good morning" (observing this woman looked really fatigued as though she had not slept well and her facial expression was as if she had the weight of the world on her shoulders); Nia asked her if she could please help her with her bags. Nia said to her in a joking kind of way, "I promise if you let me carry those bags for you, I won't run off with them." She looked at Nia with a fatigued but sweet smile and replied, "Oh, I'm not at all worried about that!"

As they were now walking side-by-side on the sidewalk, Nia observed how tired she looked. Nia asked if she could walk with her as they were approaching the physicians' entranceway. Making small talk, Nia asked if she was visiting anyone in particular and she said, "My husband!" As they entered the lobby area, the lady continued with, "My husband was in the E.D. yesterday; and was finally admitted late last night." She looked at Nia with glassy eyes and asked, "Do you think you could pray for him? He's in room 2122?" Nia was awed by her transparency and with her gentle and humble spirit. Nia responded, "It would be my pleasure to stop by. I don't know what time, but I will definitely stop by before I leave." She gave Nia a faint smile and said, "thank you." As she was walking towards the elevator, she turned around slightly and said, "Thank you, I hope you will have time to stop by." They then went in their separate directions.

Dancing with Broken Bones

Nia reported to the volunteer services office to check-in. Then she reported to the pastoral services office next door to pick up her patient lists to visit that day. Nia had three pages of patients to visit: the 2nd, 3rd, and 6th floors. The listing with the 2nd and 3rd floors only contained / listed three patients for the 2nd floor and six patients for the 3rd floor. As Nia gathered her listings and folder and several New Testament Bibles, she went back to the volunteer services office to further pack little souvenir gifts to share with patients and family members.

In her excitement, she shared with one of the volunteer services department coordinators how she met this sweet lady out on the sidewalk and how this lady so freely shared the floor and room # where her husband was located. Nia was in the process of saying to the coordinator 'I hope it's okay if I make a visit to a patient and family from a verbal invitation to visit; as she opened the folder one more time. saying to herself, "I wish her husband's name would be on my list to visit!"

It was providential. . . her husband's last name and room number was the third listed name out of four for the second floor!" Nia was covered with chill bumps and now stunned in a supernatural state of disbelief!!!!! She told the coordinator, "If I believed in spooky stuff, I would be spooked! Because that entry was NOT on that page when I looked at it over in the Pastoral Services Office!!" She shouted out loud, "How on earth did ……. (in total awe) how on earth did that just happen"? Nia had chill bumps from her head to her toes!!!!

Nia told the volunteer services coordinator, "this one (experience) is going in my journal tonight. She said she got chills too as Nia was sharing that spiritual experience. The volunteer coordinator had a regular bed pillow with the prettiest "Blessed" monogram in pink displayed on a sofa in her office. After Nia's compliments on how pretty that pillowcase was, she said "Oh, we have several that volunteers make and donate to us with various scriptures and other spiritual sayings / words". She offered Nia one to take with her to that very special 'angel' up on the 2nd floor, Room #2122.

During her visit, she shared with the patient's husband and two other family members in the room how they intersected on the sidewalk. It was absolutely the providence of God that "Nia" was the one who was chosen to meet this angel from Room 2122! What a most memorable and blessed day. This was a dance Nia would never forget!

Chapter Eleven

"Dance Burnout"

"You gotta dance like there's nobody watching,

Love like you'll never be hurt,

Sing like there's nobody listening,

And live like it's heaven on earth."

-William W. Purkey

*T*he "Dance of Love" is much more of a dialogue; one takes the lead and the other follows. One dictates a step and the other carries it out. One determines the direction, the other determines the distance traveled in a given figure. One sets the pace, the other reveals the grace. One understands the language of the other and knows what is coming next. The one leading leads with love and respect; never seeing the follower as being weak or inferior. And in the same manner, the one following follows with Trust and Submission; never feeling too big to be led or scared to jump. There is a blind assurance that someone is there to catch.

Olaotan Fawehinmi

Dance of Love Quotes

Goodreads

On a nice Sunday afternoon July 2017, a very senior yet stately friend, Mr. D. and Nia shared a mid-afternoon lunch during Restaurant Week at the Freemason Abbey Restaurant in downtown Norfolk as a "first dinner"! It was the perfect spot hidden away in our booth flirting with each other like two high school seniors on a first date. With twenty years difference between us, one of us is a baby boomer; the other is in the veteran generation. We exchanged gentle little flirtatious looks during our meal.

As the driver, I drove Mr. D. back to a family member's home (where he had been living for over a year as his health was not too good) and we watched a professional women's basketball game. Mr. D. absolutely loved the game of basketball. He was a retired basketball coach from Gallaudet University. Gallaudet University is the premier institution of learning, teaching and research for deaf and hard-of-hearing students. For more than 150 years, Gallaudet has produced leaders and innovators who have influenced history. There is no other place like this in the world. President Abraham Lincoln signed Gallaudet's charter for this comprehensive liberal arts university with the feel of a small college where its students learn in American Sign Language and English, a bilingual approach built into its mission and identity.

One Saturday afternoon, Nia and her friend were watching a movie (by happenstance) entitled, "Autumn in New York" about a New York restauranteur infamous verge-on-50 playboy, master of the no-commitment seduction until he runs into an unexpected event when he meets Charlotte Fielding. Charlotte is half Will's age and twice his match, a 21-year-old free spirit yearning to get out and taste the excitement of adult life. It is a season long encounter that will shatter Will's preconceptions about women, sex and responsibility.

Rated PG:13 Adult situation

Genre: Romance

He said, "I'm old, you're young…we have no future!" You're a kid, I'm a creep! You have better things to do than spend it with a creep like me!" Oh God my heart's already breaking. After a bitter divorce and numerous 'waste-of-my-time' relationships, Nia was in the middle of a wonderful longggg dance with what she considered a perfect gentleman: Mr. D., she asked herself, 'Suppose I fall in love with Mr. D….and he dies!' Now, my dancing is painful. My heart is emotionally bleeding: it literally hurts. Nia exclaimed, "Lord…. help me. What on earth do I do?! Do I get another dance partner or do I engage in this dance as though it is my last"?

But…it wasn't the last dance. Nia invited Mr. D to her sorority's annual formal ball that was held at the local convention center. Mr. D. was so excited about his date with Nia, with no car and no drivers license, Mr. D. took a taxi to a local tuxedo rental company. He was fitted for a tuxedo to include shoes and a hat! He paid for Nia's new ball gown, her hair and make-up appointment, and paid for her mani-pedi. She thought to herself: This is going to be an unforgettable evening.

Mr. D was no longer able to legally drive, yet he treated Nia like a princess diamond in the rough. And so Nia picked up Mr. D the morning of their big date and brought all his formal attire to her home. They dressed in separate rooms and met fully adorned in the living room. Wow…..Nia exclaimed, "I believe my ship had come in and my prince was on that ship!" It was cold that December evening and Nia wore her mother's full-length fur coat to the affair. Mr. D was just beaming with pride. He even had the audacity to have a 'lil dip in his stride…. "Go head Mr. D with your bad self!"

Once settled at their table, Nia took the initiative and invited her date to the dance floor. With some hesitation on his part, he apologized that he had not danced in years and that he felt he had two left feet. Nia wasn't taking no for an answer. As they approached the dance floor, Nia whispered to him to just let her lead the dance steps, take his time and just follow her. His face absolutely glowed with joy and excitement. Nia could only imagine this must have been how Cinderella and Prince Charming may have felt when they were together. It was the most remarkable and unforgettable evening of Nia's entire adult life! Fast forward to the spring of 2019. In spite of the current physical distance between them (five states away), it was very painful to know that Mr. D's current dance is called end-stage cancer. Nia prayed for her precious friend each and every day. This is one dance…she wished would never end.

Sadly, this dance had a very sad ending. Mr. D's disease had returned in a more aggressive manner by the end of 2019. Nia could hear his weakness over the phone. Mr. D insisted he was going to be okay and declined Nia's road trip to visit him up north. He was getting weaker and weaker. He never told her the absolute truth about his terminal illness. As an experienced clinical chaplain, Nia's guess was he was likely in hospice care and did not want her to know.

The fateful call came on February 29, 2020 (Leap year). The telephone was placed at his ear so Nia could say goodbye to her "sweet cakes". That's what he had chosen to call Nia in his stronger days; now it was her chance to return the favor. Mr. D wins the Humanitarian Award for presenting the epitome of the most angelic dancer. Nia lost her best buddy; yet Heaven gained another angel.

Chapter Twelve

"Dancing with an Angel"

"I pray that this year you're able to 'dance in the desert,' even in the face of uncertainty, fear, and chaos. For when we dance, God is faithful to bring us out."

-Bishop T.D. Jakes on Twitter

*A*s a huge binge watcher of the Hallmark Channel, Nia enjoyed a 2021 movie entitled "Sugar Plum Twist" the story of a ballerina aspiring to get the role of the Sugar Plum Fairy in "The Nutcracker". The words of wisdom from instructor to dancer: The lights, camera, the music and the stage makes it all happen. The connection between the music and the steps also makes it all happen.

The instructor's advice to the dancer… 'just because you don't get the role this time for a prima ballerina does not mean you cannot keep dancing as a role model for other young women.' Wow! What revelation; what confirmation. This story, Dancing With Broken Bones, is not just a fictional story with a character named Nia. Dancing With Broken Bones is an autobiographical snapshot of a real character who has danced through life's ups and down, challenges and successes, roadblocks and superhighways of life depicted through the nuances of the dances of life.

After 60+ years of not knowing who her biological father was Nia submitted a DNA sample given to her as a Christmas gift (2019) by her elder son Trae. DNA has confirmed Nia's real last name is "Tate; not Lucas"! This paternal dance of the unknown has finally ended.

If this transparent dance testimonial is a blessing to just one dancer's life, to God be all the Glory. Remember…just keep dancing!

Curtain Call

*S*he sits on the shore as each wave rolls and folds back into the sea. She's one with the earth's vibrations, rippling through her every fiber. It has taken time to find this calm. She has battled lifetimes to reach this place, this tranquility. Each grain of sand gives way to her every movement, unlike past troubles she had no choice but to meet head-on. But she has held fast and navigated the channels of her life to reach this place. She is peaceful now, but she knows the journey is not over. Year after year of ups and downs, laughter and heartache. But, she always moves forward, and knew eventually she would find this peace. Life is funny.... things taken, some given.... but all earned. There is knowledge that the waters will soon rise and displace this moment, as they have done so many times before, but she will move forward. It is time now, the ocean begins to kiss the tips of her toes, as the sun sets into the sea of mirrored glass. It is her time to meet her next challenge and leave this place she has deserved for so long. So, she stands to her feet and carries on, ever forward, ever strong. She will find this peace again and once more displace the sands of another shore. Ever forward.

C. Cole Vergara

What Readers are Saying...

"You have danced your way through with charm and grace. I laughed, cried, huffed and puffed and cried again. I love it."

Peggy Jackson

Administrative Officer, Retired

"What an amazing and courageous life you have led and continue to lead!"

The Reverend Anne R. Kirchmier

Rector, St. Andrew's Episcopal Church

"This memoir depicts how we can continue to dance even with damage to our most supportive structures. The dance does not stop, because if you stop there is no second act."

Sherry Burton Brown

NICU Nurse Case Manager, Retired

About The Author

Dr. Vernita Baldwin

*D*r. Vernita Baldwin is a native of Jackson, Mississippi. She is a graduate of Jackson State University with a Bachelor of Science in Business Administration; and she earned a Master of Divinity and Doctor of Ministry Degrees from the Virginia University of Lynchburg (Lynchburg VA). She is a Diamond Life Member of Delta Sigma Theta Sorority, Inc. Through the years, Dr. Baldwin continues to serve as a Lead Police Chaplain (Hampton (VA) Police Division). Her career in the field of chaplaincy has provided great experiences in spiritual support to hospice patients and families, to police officers, professional support staff and the local community. Her heart and soul is found in serving with police officers providing pastoral care behind the thin blue line. Dr. Baldwin currently serves a 4-year Hampton City Council appointment as a Faith-Based Representative on the Hampton Neighborhood Commission. Dr. Baldwin brings a wealth of experience as a chaplain, counselor, instructor, community and public service advocate. With warmth and intellect, she is a proven natural bridge-builder in civic and faith partnerships which benefit the overall health of the larger community. She finds her greatest joy in her two sons, Trae and Anthony.

Connect with the Author

Website: www.AuthorVernitaBaldwin.com

Email: dancingwithbrokenbones2023@gmail.com

Instagram: @vstyl4ever

Facebook: www.facebook.com/vernita.baldwin

LinkedIn: V. L. Baldwin, D.Min.

www.ingramcontent.com/pod-product-compliance
Lightning Source LLC
Chambersburg PA
CBHW050413030726
47503CB00006B/2170